The New Playground

by Geoff Patton
illustrated by David Clarke

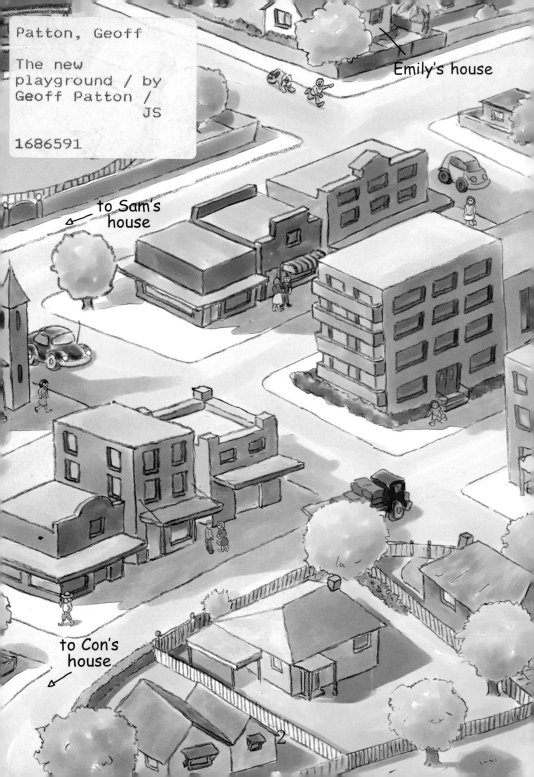

to Sam's
house

Emily's house

to Con's
house

2

Lin's apartment

Mrs Mac's farm

3

Hi. My name is Lin.
These are my neighbours.

4

Chapter 1
Flying High

Today is the day we are building the new playground. We are going to build the best playground in the whole wide world.

I ask Jenna Yoon, 'What does the best playground in the whole wide world need?'

'Swings,' says Jenna Yoon. 'Swings that go so high, when you are up, your tummy is down.'

'Yes, that's just what we need.'

We cut. We paint.
We hammer. We saw.
The swings are done.
Now we need more.

But what do we need?

Chapter 2
Watch Out for Planes

We are building the best playground in the whole wide world.

I ask Veronica Pickles, 'What does the best playground in the whole wide world need?'

'A slide,' says Veronica Pickles.
'A slide that is so high, that it needs
a flashing light on the top ... just in
case of low-flying planes.'

'Yes, that's just what we need.'

We cut. We paint.
We hammer. We saw.
The slide is done.
Now we need more.

But what do we need?

Chapter 3
101 Monkeys

We are building the best playground in the whole wide world.

I ask Emily Rimmerly, 'What does the best playground in the whole wide world need?'

'Monkey bars,' says Emily Rimmerly.
'Monkey bars that are so long, that
101 monkeys can swing all at the
same time!'

'Yes, that's just what we need.'

We cut. We paint.
We hammer. We saw.
The monkey bars are done.
Now we need more.

But what do we need?

Chapter 4
The Biggest Sandpit

We are building the best playground in the whole wide world.

I ask Toola Oola, 'What does the best playground in the whole wide world need?'

'A sandpit,' says Toola Oola.
'A sandpit that is so big that you
need to take water – just in case
you think you are lost in the
desert.'

'Yes, that's just what we need.'

We cut. We paint.
We hammer. We saw.
The sandpit is done.
Do we need more?

Chapter 5

One More Thing

We are making the best playground in the whole wide world.

I ask myself, 'What does the best playground in the whole wide world need?'

I know just what it needs ...

... all of us!

Survival Tips

1. Make sure you have lots of friends to help. You won't be able to make the best playground in the whole wide world by yourself.

2. Remember the tools. You can't make the best playground in the whole wide world without them.

3. Make sure there are no monkeys nearby or you might never get on the monkey bars!

4 Wear your goggles in the sandpit. You never know when a sandstorm might blow in.

5 Let the grown-ups build the playground, but don't let them play in it. You will never get on the swings.

Riddles and Jokes

Lin   What has no legs
but can walk?

Toola Oola   I don't know.

Lin   A pair of shoes!

Toola Oola   What runs down the street
but has no legs?

Lin   A pair of shoes?

Toola Oola   No a kerb, silly.

Lin   When is the cheapest time
to phone friends?

Emily   That's easy, when they
are not at home!

Lin   What do you call a snowman
in a desert?

Veronica   I don't know.

Lin   A puddle.